The C   W   ess

by

Oliver Richbell

Novella
Nostalgia

Published by City Fiction

Copyright © 2019 Oliver Richbell

ISBN: 978-1-910040-24-9

Sarah Tomkins said "No!" and had meant it. She pleaded with the prosecuting barrister, Amanda Buckingham, to believe her. Amanda feared that some of the jury had already made up their minds that Sarah had consented, and they would find the two accused men not guilty.

The trial had not gone well for Amanda, one of the rising stars of the Bar. She knew she was going to have to face her own demons for Sarah to get what she was so desperate for — justice..

THE COURAGEOUS WITNESS

It was a size too big for her. That was why she was wearing it.

Amanda wrapped the pink-flowered cheongsam around her naked body. In the privacy of her Clerkenwell flat, in the hour past midnight, she felt secure in the protective 'long shirt'. She was sipping hot water which, according to ancient Chinese medicine, stimulated blood flow around the body and had restorative healing qualities. She had a throbbing headache and was ready to try anything to shift it.

Amanda curled up on her sofa which was far too big for her flat. She was not comfortable but staying in the foetal position seemed to ease her stress. She was reading a policy document produced by the Crown Prosecution Service. After yawning, she stood up and stretched her aching limbs. She walked into her kitchen to check that Rumpole's water bowl was full. As she did so, she glanced at the digital clock on her oven. With a sigh, Amanda knew she had to go to bed if she was to function in the morning, but she was acutely aware that the last hour or so of reading had been mostly ineffectual – unless by some sheer miracle she had retained information through osmosis.

Filling Rumpole's water bowl and sprinkling a perfect dozen cat biscuits into his favourite bowl, Amanda focused her mind on the CPS document about the prosecution of rape cases:

Rape is one of the most serious of all criminal offences. It can inflict lasting trauma on victims and their families.

and

The majority of rape victims are women and most know their rapist.

Sarah Tomkins certainly knew the two men charged with her assault. She knew them extremely well.

Rape also has a devastating effect on families of the victims.

Amanda returned to the sofa, lost in memories that sent a shiver through her. She shook her head to try to push them deep back inside. With a groan of discomfort as her headache refused to ease, she returned to the papers.

The CPS realises that victims of rape have difficult decisions to make that will affect their lives and the lives of those close to them.

Amanda had read all of the evidence several times previously and she was still unsure as to why Sarah was refusing anonymity and was focusing on her day in court. Amanda concluded that Sarah was after revenge – and public revenge at that.

The law does not require the victim to have resisted physically in order to prove lack of consent. The question of whether the victim consented is a matter for the jury to decide.

Amanda looked up from her laptop and stared straight ahead as she recited the provisions of The Sexual Offences Act 2003;

The defendant must show that his belief in consent was reasonable.

Amanda was thinking hard and had almost forgotten about her headache. She turned back to the CPS document and decided to reread what she felt certain was the most important passage of all:

Proving the absence of consent is usually the most difficult part of a rape prosecution and is the most common reason for a rape case to fail. Prosecutors will look for evidence such as injury, struggle or immediate distress to help them.

Amanda's immediate challenge was clear, unlike her head that was now beset with a thick fog because of the absolute refusal of her headache to ease. She was simply unable to shake her belief that it was going to be difficult – very difficult – to convince a jury that Sarah Tomkins was the victim of a sexual assault by two men and, in the case of one of them, rape. Amanda was racked by tormented memories that she could no longer repress. Despite her sub-conscious efforts, these were racing around her pulsating head like fireflies and she was struggling to concentrate.

You'll feel better after a good night's sleep was always the advice from her Aunt Eileen. There was no chance of a good night's sleep and Amanda knew it. Her brain was aching as it leapt from thought to thought but, with each passing moment, she started to lose the last remnants of focus as she began to muddle the facts of Sarah Tomkins' case with her own bitter memories.

Amanda fell onto her bed and underwent the fight with the duvet and the scatter cushions as she struggled to get comfortable. Eventually, after a considerable and over-elaborate effort, she was able to wiggle herself down and under the covers. Following two meaningful punches to her pillows, she finally closed her eyes.

A second or so after doing so, a thought came to her. Had she fed Rumpole? She couldn't remember but she knew that if she hadn't, he'd be walking all over her and purring into her ear in just a few minutes.

Amanda kicked the covers off. With a loud cry of

"Diu!" (Cantonese for "fuck!"), she stomped into the kitchen. In the half-light of the London night she could see her pet with his face in his food bowl, scoffing his late evening meal.

Amanda spun on her heels and went back to bed but was not quite as comfortable as before. She was giving in to exhaustion – but then the events that haunted her earlier began to replay in her mind.

He had come up behind her, totally unexpectedly. Despite her judo training from Fat Freddie in Kowloon, she was helpless as he forced her over.

Rumpole came and joined Amanda on the bed, curling up between her knees and elbows. She, though half asleep, placed a hand over his stomach. She failed to realise from his breathing patterns that not all was well with her fat cat.

A few weeks earlier, Sarah Tomkins had been lying prostrate on her back on the boardroom table. She could feel the hard surface irritating the skin of her buttocks. Eddie was penetrating her as Ivan, watching from the side, was gathering his breath and pulling up his trousers.

"She likes it rough," he gasped. "Have your fill, Eddie."

Sarah was numb; her mind had switched off and she was unable to register anything. She lay powerless with Eddie – sweaty, odious and panting – on top of her. Around the boardroom were cheap, non-matching chairs that had been upturned around the room a few minutes earlier.

The table and chairs belonged to a vehicle distribution company. It dealt in sales and its management meetings focused on sales figures. It didn't matter that the room lacked warmth and nothing matched or showed a co-ordinated brand identity. Craig Heaton, the company's founder and chairman, didn't care. He only cared about profit and he had a fierce reputation for sacking staff for not reaching their often almost impossible targets.

Ivan was a senior salesman at Heaton Van Sales. He had brought in a significant order – worth close to a half million pounds – for supplying a fleet of custom transit vans. His success had been announced in the very room he was now getting dressed in, and which resulted in an impromptu party that had started three hours earlier in the staff kitchen on the ground floor of Heaton House.

Eddie, Ivan's devoted subordinate, had supported him faithfully like a lap-dog throughout the four months of endless negotiations up to the contract being signed. The order invoiced out at £488,887. Ivan's bonus was 5% of the total, so a smidgen under £24,500 of which he gave £4,000 to Eddie, £1,500 to Luca, an assistant salesman (who played a key role in securing the deal), £400 to Sarah and £200 each to her three colleagues on reception. Ivan still cleared almost £18,000 on one order and this was on top of his basic pay.

When Craig, who was at his beachside apartment in the Canary Islands, heard that the customer had paid in full, he walked round the swimming pool with a bottle of champagne, making sure that everyone knew he had landed another deal. It was, of course, down to him as usual, he boasted, but in reality he didn't even know the names of some of his staff, let alone the precise details of the deals they were doing. It was always about the bottom line with him; about the money in the bank, nothing else. His reply to London was short but exultant:

'Brilliant performance. It's party time: no limits. C.'

Craig liked to sign off every internal email, message or memorandum with a capital C. However, it didn't stand for Craig but for chairman. It was important that everyone knew he was in charge even though he was rarely in the office. As he sat down on one of the empty loungers around his beachfront apartment he cast a disinterested look over the beach. A semi-naked bathing beauty turned over on her sunbed and he found himself wondering if Sarah would hang around for the party he'd just authorised. He liked Sarah; he even recalled her name. Mind you, most men who met her didn't quickly forget her.

His thoughts about Sarah slowly disappeared. After all, he'd never make it back in time for the party. As he turned back away from the splendid sea view, his gold signet ring sparkled in the late afternoon sun. People always assumed that the jewel-encrusted C stood for Craig. It didn't, of course; it stood for chairman.

Back at Heaton Van Sales, alcohol and food had been delivered by the same high-end grocery business that had just agreed their order for a fleet of transit vans. Ivan told everyone who would listen that it was his order. Luca didn't mind; after all, no-one in the office would believe him over Ivan anyway, and it was better to be with Ivan than against him.

As is traditional at office parties, there was far more booze than food. It was not clear who brought in the 'powder'. The repair shop was the likely source although, with the appearance of a number of 'guests' including blonds, brunettes and redheads, their later protests of innocence were accepted. As it was, a few of the staff spent more time in the toilets than they did dancing in the foyer and on the kitchen tables. The women on reception sorted the music by setting up a playlist on a smart phone.

Their office celebrations were quite regular events but Ivan was keen to make this, one to remember. He wanted everyone to know that he was a dynamic salesman and his parties were the best, especially as Craig was not there to steal his thunder.

There was booze, some food, music, drugs and girls: the party had begun.

Sarah was the head receptionist. She had helped to transform her team into an efficient, professional 'front-facing' part of the Heaton Van Sales machine. She always paid close attention to her appearance and she insisted that all 'her girls' did likewise. Her mantra was: "We are the first people customers see. We must greet them with courtesy and politeness, and always look professional". It would never be the catchphrase of the year, but she really did believe it.

It helped that she and 'her girls' regarded themselves as good-looking. In her case, that was not in question.

Sarah was enjoying the party; she always did. She stayed away from the coke – it wasn't her thing, and never had been, but she accepted that others partook. She had joined in the dancing with enthusiasm, eating little of what was on offer but drinking a lot of vodka and tonic. She was currently without a serious partner. She was happy to wait for one and to date casually in the interim.

Everyone knew that Sarah liked Ivan and Ivan

liked Sarah. The flirtatious banter that passed between them over the receptionists' desk was devoid of subtlety most of the time and occasionally was downright lascivious. Neither seemed too fussed that Ivan was married with a child.

As the early evening celebrations began to unravel into the usual drunken shenanigans, Sarah, who had danced with Ivan a lot, at times very closely indeed, suggested to him that they have a more private party. She had surveyed her colleagues who were either wobbly, playing tonsil hockey or hurrying back and forth to the toilets, and had decided that it was time for a bit of fun. He was not exactly a 'newbie' to adultery and did not need any encouragement.

They slipped away from the mayhem and headed for the stairs that led to the boardroom. Ivan gestured for Eddie to come with him.

The fourth of their little group was the ever-present Luca. Apart from running around getting them drinks and taking away their empties, he'd never been more than six feet away from Ivan from the moment the music started. Ivan caught Luca's eye and mouthed "Piss off" to him, gesturing back towards the party.

Ivan and Sarah were giggling like teenagers as they stumbled and fumbled the stairs. Eddie was half a dozen steps behind them, trying to catch a glimpse of forbidden flesh up Sarah's skirt. Against the wall by the boardroom door, Ivan and Sarah began to embrace. There was no element of sensitivity or subtlety; it was simply animalistic desire.

Eddie walked past them both and into the boardroom.

Sarah and Ivan stopped. Wiping her mouth with

the back of her hand Sarah gasped,

"Get rid of him, Ivan, now!"

"We're a team, Sarah, me and Eddie. You've had your bonus – now it's our turn."

He pushed her into the boardroom, grabbing her backside as he did so.

"That's a fine bit of ass you've got there," he crowed, kicking the door behind him.

As it banged shut, Eddie slurred,

"Remember the porn we watched the other night? Those two blokes and the nurse."

"It wasn't as good as that Japanese lot in the sauna," roared Ivan, high-fiving Eddie.

Sarah was sobering up – and was becoming concerned. She went for the door but, before she could escape, found herself being dragged back across the room and held down on the table. Eddie and Ivan pulled at her clothes. She cried out as her bra was ripped off.

"Please, no," she pleaded.

"I'll go first," growled Ivan as he pulled down her knickers.

Eddie held her as his colleague wiggled down his trousers. Sarah could not understand how Ivan, who she had really fancied, could be metamorphosing into the hefty, panting lump now forcing himself on top of her. She didn't try to resist. She couldn't, as every ounce of fight she thought she had vanished in the sheer terror of the moment. Ivan then had sex with her and slid off the table.

Sarah felt Eddie's grip on her arms relax. She opened her eyes. Eddie loomed up in front of her. Sarah feared that he was going to rape her. Desperately, she tried to climb away but he pushed her down on to the wooden surface. Her head crashed against the frame.

"No!" she screamed aloud.

When she tried to scream again, one of the men shoved his hand into her face. She struggled, but he was too strong for her. Sarah fought back and managed a split second of freedom which was just long enough for her to gasp for air. The next thing she felt was a fist hitting the side of her head. She winced in pain and momentarily lost consciousness. Then the hand returned to her mouth more brutally than before. The tears were uncontrollable as she felt herself being penetrated.

Summoning all her strength she made one final effort to escape but the two men just shoved her back down with the same care they'd treat an overfull wheelie bin.

Panicking, she opened her eyes and saw Ivan watching her, leering, his face sweaty and red.

"Fuck her good, Eddie," he screeched.

Sarah began to shake with revulsion.

Eddie withdrew. He then ran both his hands up her legs and pinched her inner thighs. Sarah's eyes bulged and she yelled out in pain. Eddie laughed and squeezed her flesh again.

Sarah turned her head to one side and tried to retch. Ivan grabbed Eddie and said, "Nice one, mate. You head back down, I'll be down in five."

Ivan moved back to Sarah and tried to re-arrange her blouse. Wild-eyed, Sarah fended him off with frantic hands. She slid off the table, so she was leaning against it, and pulled down her skirt. One of her bra straps had broken, but she managed to fasten the buttons on her blouse. Her shoes were a few feet in front of her.

Ivan suggested, "Let's get back to the party."

Sarah stopped dead in her tracks with one hand on the back of a poorly-veneered wooden chair. She stared at him in utter disbelief as her contempt began to show.

"You do what you want, but I'm calling the police," she said.

Ivan laughed.

"Will you tell them you were first up the stairs?" he mocked.

"You and your fucking sidekick attacked me," she said.

Ivan laughed again. With more than just a hint of disdain in his voice, he told her that he was going for a drink and, when she came to her senses, she was welcome to join him.

Sarah watched with her hand on the chair as she tried to regain her balance. He sauntered out of the room without another word to her. The sound of that metallic click as the door closed would be one she would never forget.

She slumped onto the seat and grimaced from an internal pain. She had been gripping the chair for what seemed like an age. Her hands were shaking and she felt cold. The pain was beginning to ease. After a few moments, that felt like hours, she slowly rose to her feet. She tried to straighten her hair and wipe away her smeared lipstick. She pulled down her blouse and tried to remove some of the creases. She then turned and, with a deliberate but feigned poise, she took a few steps to the door.

She stepped out into the landing and inched her way to the top of the stairs and stopped. There was more pain and a lot of spasms were hitting her. They seemed to wash over her like a boat swallowed by a gigantic wave. It was then that she realised there was blood running down her inner thighs.

She gripped the banister with her left hand but was feeling light-headed. She wobbled at the top of the staircase and started to fall. In a flash, Luca caught her without a second to spare.

"Oh, mother of mercy," he cried, as Sarah collapsed into his protective arms.

Thirty-five minutes later, Sarah was admitted to the Accident and Emergency Department of Nailton Hospital, having been assessed by a Police Examiner. The doctor inserted three stitches into her perineum, which was ripped, and prescribed a course of antibiotics. When her blood pressure dropped back to an acceptable level, she was discharged with orders to return the next day for further checks to be made. Her mother and step-father had responded to a call from the hospital admissions desk and were together in the waiting room wanting to take her home. As the maternal arms wrapped around her, Sarah whispered into her mother's ear: "Mum, they fucking raped me!"

Back at Heaton Van Sales, the party had come to abrupt end after the ambulance had taken Sarah to hospital. The gossip-mill was turning fast. The police questioned everyone present and recorded their full names and contact details before they were allowed to leave.

The Detective Inspector had arrived and his team had surveyed and catalogued the chaotic remnants of the party: food trodden into the floor; bins overflowing with empty beer cans, wine and spirit bottles; and the pungent smell of stale alcohol that hung in the air like an odious fog. Those who had partaken in other party accessories were paranoid beyond belief and probably brought more unwanted attention upon themselves by their furtive, twitching faces. The police were not interested in that aspect. They concentrated their investigations on the initial questioning of Ivan, Eddie and Luca. All the members of the reception desk were keen to make statements. At around eleven o'clock the Detective Inspector cautioned Ivan and Eddie and arrested them on suspicion of aggravated assault and rape.

There was only one topic of conversation throughout the office on Monday. Sarah did not report for work and Ivan and Eddie were missing. Craig was furious in having to have spent a lot of time dealing with Yvette, the personnel director, over the weekend. She laid out the factual and legal position to the chairman and notified Ivan and Eddie that they were suspended, pending the outcome of the police inquiry together with an internal company investigation. Craig was mainly concerned with the costs involved and whether the incident could depress sales.

Some weeks later, Amanda Buckingham was feeling the lump in Rumpole's belly. She felt awful. She'd always been diligent about getting him checked out when he had been ill but, this time, engrossed in her work and thoughts, she kept forgetting to book an appointment.

An hour later, the on-duty vet was ruffling Rumpole's head. Amanda's stomach turned; *one phone call was all I needed to have made so why did it take me so long to do it!* Her pet licked the vet's hand.

"I've been so irresponsible," said Amanda.

"No, not at all, don't be too hard on yourself," replied the vet, Ben Lister. Ben smiled at her reassuringly and made eye contact. Amanda held his gaze for several moments and then he broke away with an over-elaborate, "Anyway...back to Rumpole."

She had met him on several occasions when taking the cat for his injections and regular check-ups. Ben often teased Amanda with the suggestion that she should receive a loyalty card for the number of visits she accumulated in a year. Rumpole was nine years old which, in human terms, was around sixty-five years.

The vet's good looks were not lost on Amanda – and nor were hers on him. He had, at one of their earlier encounters, nodded with respect and interest when Amanda dropped into conversation that she was a barrister. Since then he teased her about her profession and told her the name for the cat was cute but a little obvious.

Amanda seldom missed signals. She was trained to read people and was blessed with an above average gift of intuition. For once, she merely took Ben's interest as part of the bedside manner. She later made a conscious effort to pay more attention to Ben's non-cat chat.

The vet was studying a scan of the lump in Rumpole's stomach. Amanda caught his gaze. He looked up.

"Yes, it's as I thought," and, with a slight pause for dramatic effect as Amanda held her breath, continued, "it's a cat."

He smiled and Amanda laughed.

"It's not too critical," he diagnosed, after a moment or so of careful deliberation.

"Too?" was the word that Amanda heard and repeated.

Perhaps, somewhat unprofessionally, he walked over to her and put his arm around her shoulders; it seemed, somehow, acceptable. She felt him squeeze her.

"You say he's had no food since late last night so we'll take the lump out later today," he said, "and then, I'm afraid, it's in the hands of Saint Gertrude." He smiled at Amanda who seemed bemused. "Saint Gertrude is the patron saint of cats," he added.

"If it's cancer?" she asked.

"We'll send the lump for biopsy, and we'll find that out later. The first priority is to remove the growth and get him stable and comfortable," said Ben.

"What are his chances?" she asked.

"If Ben Lister is operating, better than most," quipped the vet.

Amanda appreciated the further effort at light-heartedness. Ben put Rumpole into his cage and he buzzed for a nurse to take him away.

"You go off and win your case and I'll fight on here," he suggested. "I'll text you when I have some news." He stared at her. "We'll do our best for him," he said.

"You and Saint Gertrude," said Amanda.

From her early days as a barrister, the Head of Hartington Chambers, located in Lincoln's Inn in central London, had taken a special interest in the niece of his friend, Anthony Buckingham.

As Amanda was sitting directly in front of Rufus Hetherington-Jones QC, she was being circumspect in reflecting her annoyance.

"Firstly, Rufus, I defend – so why have I received a prosecution brief?" she asked.

"We take what we're given," responded the Head of Chambers. "You know that is the way it works." He then repeated his favourite adage. "You know what I always say, Amanda: 'It is better to have your hand up than out'."

Nodding impatiently, Amanda continued her objections.

"Secondly, and after my review of the papers, I understand why the CPS is bringing this case to court but I've got some concerns. I am not sure how I can convince a jury that she did not consent. She led the way to the boardroom. She allowed sex to take place with the first man and, although she claims she said "No", she still had sex with the second one. She cannot explain why she allowed this man to remain in the room at the beginning or why she did not protest when the door was locked. She must have realised that they intended to have sex with her." She raised her eyebrows as she awaited Rufus' reply.

Amanda was taking out her frustration, at the brief she had been presented with, on her Head of Chambers. This was not usually a wise course of action for any barrister at Hartington to follow. However, given the nature of their relationship, she was allowed a certain degree of latitude which was not afforded to any of her peers – and most certainly not to her colleague, with whom she shared a room, Mr

Trevor Hamper-Houghton.

As the two barristers continued to debate the case, the usual hum of activity, in and around the Clerk's room, was beginning to wane as other members of Chambers and staff were passively listening to the conversation while trying to appear, and in the most failing, to look busy. They were enjoying the verbal back and forth as the barristers traded shots in a game of intellectual tennis.

Rufus, noting that they were becoming a distraction, waved Amanda into one of empty conference rooms. As he did so he caught the eye of Hartington Chambers' practice manager, a seasoned clerk by the name of David Blyth. David was a 'Dave' from Essex who had clerked his way up the ranks and, whilst he called himself Dave, Rufus always referred to him as David.

Rufus had no problem talking through any issue with anyone at chambers and he liked the paternal persona he thought he cultivated. Not all, if any, agreed that he generated this very well. However, no-one ever told him and so Rufus's belief in his own 'father-figure' status remained a constant source of amusement within chambers and no more so than to Dave and the rest of the support staff.

Amanda dutifully followed him into the conference room. Rufus closed the door. She sat down without waiting to be asked as she could feel her inner tension mounting. She decided to speak first.

"Rufus, let me summarise the position." She lingered for a second or so, allowing Rufus to take a seat opposite her, and so she could re-gather her momentum lost by the change of scenery. "Sarah

Tomkins was one of the leaders in organising the office party. She had, by her own admission, drunk a lot of alcohol. There were drugs on hand but there is no suggestion that she used them. She went willingly with Ivan, and his associate Eddie Delaney, to the boardroom away from the party. She, in her own statement, claimed she protested that Eddie was there but, nevertheless, had consensual intercourse with Ivan. Her clothes were ripped but there is nothing to suggest she resisted at that point."

Rufus leant into the middle of the table and opened a bottle of expensive bottled water. He poured himself and Amanda a glass each. He then sat back, awaiting the next volley.

Amanda nodded her thanks. Moving the glass in front of her, she didn't wait for a coaster – much to the annoyance of Rufus. She carried on.

"Now, this is where matters get even more complicated. Eddie alleges he was encouraged by Sarah to have sex with her; she says she said "No". Sarah then claimed that someone hit her on the side of her head, but the Police Examiner reported no bruising. Sex occurred, the accused say, with consent, Sarah says the opposite."

Rufus, having had little to say so far, finished his glass of water with an audible smack of his lips. Sarah moved on, ignoring the noise.

"The two men then abandoned her and return to the party. Sarah found her own way out of the room, discovered she was bleeding, and collapsed. Luckily, Luca Toskas caught her. She was taken to hospital where she had three stitches to her perineum and was prescribed antibiotics."

She hesitated momentarily and looked down at her

notes.

"Ivan was charged with sexual assault and Eddie with sexual assault and rape. I gather that the CPS considered charging Ivan with rape as well but they subsequently dropped that charge against him because there was not sufficient evidence."

Amanda drained her glass, this time placing it neatly in the centre of her coaster. She looked at Rufus. He returned eye contact and Amanda concluded with, "They are both, without a doubt, guilty."

"So, prove it and get a conviction," said the Head of Hartington Chambers in a rather matter-of-fact tone.

"I can't prove either of the charges and the defence counsel will slaughter Sarah in the witness box."

"And you lose a case," interjected Rufus.

"I can live with that, Rufus, but I don't want the see the woman destroyed."

Carefully, and with a degree of sensitivity, he responded.

"Right, Amanda, let's take a step back and focus on what you have in your favour?"

Amanda snapped, "You mean in Sarah's favour, surely!"

Rufus recoiled back in his chair, with his arms out in front of him, in surrender.

He did not understand what Amanda said next because it was mumbled and certainly not in English.

With a slight air of apology, she smiled.

"Sorry, Rufus. Cantonese."

It broke the tension. Laughing in reply, Rufus added, "I can speak French."

"Eh bien," countered Amanda.

The two barristers sat silently for a moment until Amanda declared, "I can certainly present enough evidence, but it is about how the jury view Ivan and Edward. Ivan is a father and has a pregnant partner. Eddie, from the statements on file, is the more aggressive personality but they both maintain that sex with Sarah was consensual."

"The CPS is bringing the case, not you, Amanda," declared Rufus, "and you cannot get emotionally involved." He wondered if he was being too cold-hearted and tried to back-track. "The CPS is to lead and prepare the evidence and your job is to present it in the best way and then allow the jury to decide the outcome."

That was the end of the conversation, Amanda was not really sure if the discussion had been of any use but she was grateful Rufus had at least listened to her. She followed him to the door and, as he politely ushered her out of the conference room, her mobile phone vibrated.

She walked a few paces and then read the message. *'Op in 30 mins. R is peaceful. B.'*

Amanda sat with the CPS officer and went through the police files, the evidence and the charges. They had a lot of work to do. Inwardly, Amanda lacked confidence in the case but the CPS was optimistically bullish. While they waited for Sarah Tomkins to arrive, Amanda decided to express her reservations. The CPS solicitor was indifferent. "We have passed the threshold test," was the 'stock' response. Amanda raised her concerns from a professional standpoint; personally, she felt a sense of unease and impending defeat.

Sarah Tomkins arrived and was ushered into the meeting room by a male caseworker, perhaps in his early twenties who, incredibly, 'checked out' Sarah's behind as he closed the door. Amanda noticed this with a sense of utter incredulity that she only just managed to keep to herself. It was with a heavy heart that she smiled at Sarah as she sat down at the table.

She was wearing a blue top, pressed jeans, sandals and her hair was cut short.

"I'm here, Sarah, to understand your position and to prepare the Crown's case," she began.

"Thank you," interjected Sarah, "but, please, no legal niceties; there is no need."

" OK," she replied. She waited as Sarah rummaged in her bag. She put two pieces of menthol chewing gum into her mouth and began to chew. Amanda understood that this was her signal to press on and go to work.

The meeting lasted for several hours. Sarah was composed throughout and responded honestly to Amanda's detailed questions. The CPS solicitor added much to the conversation about how Sarah would give her evidence at the forthcoming trial. Sarah and the CPS solicitor had discussed and agreed that she would not seek any special measures in relation to the giving of evidence. Amanda was impressed with the courageous approach being taken by Sarah.

After the meeting ended, and on her journey back to Chambers, she reflected on what Sarah had said. The conclusion was the same as it had been earlier in the day: this case was going to test the barrister to the limits of her abilities.

Later that afternoon, Amanda was in her office, poring over the case file and her notes from the meeting. Papers were strewn across the table, on the floor and on the windowsill behind her. Post-it notes of all shapes, sizes and colours protruded from all angles making, to the untrained eye, her desk seem like a primary school art collage. Amanda felt comforted by the effort she was putting in and she gained some reassurance that, at the very least, she was going to be well prepared for trial.

She sensed her mobile phone vibrate on her desk. Searching through papers and bundles and text books she finally located it hidden between the pages of her notepad.

She read the message received:

'Op over. R rather poorly. Sorry. B.'

She read the message again. She drafted a response but didn't send it. She placed her mobile into her bag and returned to her paperwork.

Amanda spent Sunday afternoon with Trevor Hamper-Houghton. He was courteous, funny and well-informed. He asked her for another 'pre-date date' as he liked to call their irregular gatherings. She agreed to meet him again the following Saturday and he suggested taking the Eurostar to Brussels for a day trip. She wondered if she had shown him sufficient enthusiasm as he clumsily back-tracked in fear of being rejected.

The truth of the matter was that Amanda's mind was preoccupied with the upcoming case. Her preoccupation with Sarah's innocence continued to invade her rather cramped brain. The preliminary hearing was set for Monday. If the defendants didn't have a Road to Damascus bout of conscience, the matter would be listed for trial at Crown Court.

Monday came and went. The two defendants confirmed their respective names and their pleas of 'not guilty'. Sarah was not present. This entire episode lasted a matter of minutes and was, at best, perfunctory.

Amanda had her routines as well as her quirks. On the morning of each new trial she did two things. She rose early and went to the gym. Her personal trainer, Zach, was quite amenable to this routine as Amanda was paying well over the odds. Although he kept his thoughts to himself, he relished the look of Amanda in Lycra kit. She liked to box before a trial; pad work, mainly, but she found it far more rewarding than a normal gym session. The second of her pre-trial rituals was a real indulgence. It was a full-fat cappuccino with chocolate sprinkles from her favourite coffee shop just off Lincoln's Inn Square.

She sat in her room at Chambers, a dank, mouldy old pump room in the bowels of the Old Square. The clerks had told her it was only a temporary office but that had been several years ago. Energised by her gym work-out and a warm feeling inside as she devoured her cappuccino extravaganza, Amanda was ready.

With a clenched fist of delight as she three-pointed her immaculately drained take-away cup into the waste paper bin, Amanda picked up her trolley bag that she had carefully packed. The handle was grabbed and, with a hefty tug, given the weight of the paper inside, she strode away. Amanda walked assertively passed the other 'temporary' residents of her floor. Her office door had closed with a thud and inside it was now almost completely dark, save for the neon glow of the phone that had been left on her desk.

A few moments later, Amanda re-entered her office and grabbed her mobile, stuffing it into her coat pocket. She then left for a second time, with a renewed determination to win the case.

Nailton Crown Court was as inspiring as a Stalinist gulag in the depths of winter. It lacked warmth, charm and architectural appeal. "Buildings can be warm and inviting," thought Amanda, but this court edifice was neither, especially as the heating was unreliable.

In the robing room, Amanda donned her black gown and short wig. It wasn't a flattering look for anyone but she quite liked the history and the tradition behind it. Walking into court, with a bow of the head as she entered, she took her place next to her trolley bag. Meticulously she laid out her papers, notes and pens. She poured herself a beaker full of tepid tap water that had been placed in a plastic jug by the court clerk.

There was nothing else she needed to do. She was ready. She was Amanda Buckingham, prosecution counsel.

Unlike scenes from Hollywood movies, British jury selection consists of a series of random ballots. First you are summoned, then you are allocated an alpha-numeric reference and placed into a pool. Fifteen of your pool colleagues then attend before the judge and the court where a final lottery takes place. If your number comes up you take one of the twelve seats. It's like a bizarre game of musical chairs, without music, levity or a prize, pondered Amanda. She, even as a junior member of Chambers, had seen too many jury formations to easily recall each in detail but, every time, the sheer randomness never disappointed her. She was not a football fan but, as she watched the jurors-in-waiting being called as jurors, and taking their seats in two banks of six, Amanda likened the process to those halcyon days of cup draws with stiff, crusty old farts pulling numbered balls out of silk bags.

Assessing the final twelve members of the jury was an essential element of the criminal legal process, whether you are defending or prosecuting. Amanda hoped that she would be fortunate with the final make-up. Inwardly, she prayed for more women than men to be on the jury. She reasoned that women would be more empathetic towards Sarah.

The final composition of the jury was six men and six women.

"It could have been worse," she said to herself.

Judge Clarke went through his usual repartee. He was a solid and well-respected man but he had certain peccadilloes. Amanda had been before him on several previous occasions. While he would never tolerate questioning off the beaten path, he had always allowed her some degree of latitude. Judge Clarke reminded the jury of their serious and civic duties in painstaking detail. Some of the jury were already lost; others took frantic notes; one looked half-asleep. When he had finished with the jury he turned to public gallery.

Amanda sat watching the jury, looking for eye contact. She caught two or three sets of eyes and smiled back – not a teeth flasher, but a professional smile with a slight nod.

Sarah's mother and step-father sat quietly together in the gallery. They were surrounded by friends of the defendants and a few unknowns who were looking for some enthralling courtroom jousting. There was a law student present – he was obviously a student as his legal text books were by his side together with a cheap-looking packet sandwich.

The only other person left in the room was Archie Morton, an experienced bulldog of a defence counsel. He had made a good living in defending criminal cases; his motto (and that of Waitland Chambers where he had practised and honed his craft for two decades) was, *'If they pay, we'll plead nay'*.

Amanda really didn't like him at all, even on a professional level. He was fixated by money and the 'Holy Grail' of becoming a QC. There was no altruism, no public interest, no soul to Archie Morton; this did, however, make him a formidable opponent and Amanda knew she would have to be at the top of her game from the off.

During a long and tedious narrative from Judge Clarke, Archie did nothing other than assess and scan the jury. He was slick, like slow-moving oil, and just as toxic, but for some reason, he often managed to get jury members on his side. He nodded to some, smiled at others and stared others out.

All of this administration and ground rules meant that Judge Clarke decided on an early lunch; the jury looked relieved and funnelled out of the courtroom. The two defendants seemed confused at this unexpected halt in proceedings. Eventually, the court room emptied save for Archie and Amanda.

"Well then, Buckers," sneered Morton, "I see you are playing with the other side of the bat on this one." He continued the cricket analogies. "The wicket's no good for you, I'm afraid, and there's no chance of this going five days."

Amanda didn't follow cricket and so Morton's words were lost on her. She had to respond, albeit ineffectively.

"I'm happy to take this one on," she stammered.

She finished packing away her papers into her trolley bag and left the courtroom.

After an uninspiring lunch with the CPS solicitor, Amanda opened the Crown's case against Mr Ivan Derbyshire and Mr Edward Delaney. Every single word had been revised, reviewed, amended, modified and triple-checked. Amanda delivered her speech perfectly. Her tone was spot on and the tempo was even better. Silence is such a powerful tool in any successful advocate's arsenal and Amanda let every detail of the events that had taken place in the Heaton Van Sales boardroom hang in the air like poisoned arrows. There was a deathly silence as they landed on the jury.

Archie, however, had seen this coming. By the time he'd dissected Amanda's opening comments, the visitor in the gallery was perplexed. What would the verdict be? At the end of day one, the law student summarised his notes with two words: Not Guilty.

Day two saw the start of witness evidence. The first person called took the oath and confirmed that his name was Luca Gabor Toskas. He stated that his parents had brought him and his sister to live in the United Kingdom in the 1990s. He said that he had joined Heaton Van Sales three years ago and was part of Ivan's team. Luca made it clear that he liked his job very much.

He then went through the events of the Friday evening, when the alleged assault took place, and confirmed that he had followed Ivan, Eddie and Sarah up the stairs. Ivan had told him to go back to the party. He said that he did not mind because a pretty blonde girl was waiting for him.

He categorically denied taking any drugs but confirmed that they were available but the source of such were unknown to him.

"So, Mr Toskas, how far up the stairs did you climb?" asked Amanda.

"To the first floor," he replied.

"And that was the point when Mr Derbyshire told you to return to the party."

"Yes."

"What did he say?" asked Amanda.

"He made it clear that I was not welcome," replied Luca.

"What words did he use, Mr Toskas?"

The assistant salesman looked around him, unsure if he was allowed to swear an oath and in court. Amanda read the situation and placated the witness with a smile.

"He told me to piss off," he stuttered.

There was a snigger around the court room. Judge Clarke raised one of his bushy eyebrows in annoyance and gently tapped his bench with his left-hand knuckles to let everyone know he had heard the laughter and that it was not permitted in *his* court.

Amanda repeated, "'Piss off'…do you think that is a friendly way to be spoken to, Mr Toskas?"

"It's the way he always speaks to me," he replied.

"I can imagine," she acknowledged, glancing at Judge Clarke. He'd heard her comment, but, thankfully, let it slide. Archie was texting under the table, so he missed her unprofessional remark.

Amanda noticed that two of the six women who made up the jury were fidgeting and exchanging nods of agreement.

"Did you immediately return to the party?" enquired Amanda.

"Yes. You can be sure. I'm olive-skinned. The girls love us Europeans."

There was at least one laugh from the gallery. The student looked around but all heads had dropped like a mass prayer had been called. Judge Clarke imperiously scowled at where the noise had come from. Waiting for the nod from the judge, Amanda stood still. The approval came and she began again.

"So, you returned to the party?"

"Yes."

"Therefore, you have no idea what happened to Mr Derbyshire, Mr Delaney and Miss Tomkins," countered Amanda.

"We all know what happened," said Luca.

"How do you know?" pounced Amanda.

"Well...I don't. I wasn't there," stammered Luca.

"Thank you, Mr Toskas," interrupted Amanda, "we have your evidence that you were not there. Now, I want to ask you about the events that happened later. This was when Miss Tomkins collapsed into your arms. This took place on the third floor?"

"At the bottom of the stairs leading up to the boardroom," Luca said.

"On the third floor," said Amanda.

"Yes."

"What were you doing there?" she asked.

"I have explained. Ivan and Eddie are my friends. I wanted to make sure they were having fun."

The courtroom fell into a brief period of silence as Amanda waited for Luca to keep talking. After a few moments it was apparent that he would not; Amanda then rallied.

"So, what about the girl at the party?" asked Amanda.

"I don't understand you," said Luca.

Amanda debated explaining the point but she hesitated.

"You went up the stairs and you caught Miss Tomkins."

"Yes. There was blood on her hand."

"Yes, thank you, Mr Toskas. We will come to that shortly," declared Amanda. She paused and wrote that down on her notepad.

"You must have passed Mr Derbyshire and Mr Delaney on their way down the stairs then?" Amanda asked.

"Just Ivan," he said. "We passed as he went back into the party."

Luca ran his hand through his hair and fiddled with his tie. He went for the water and gulped down a large cup full.

"Mr Delaney was upstairs," stated Amanda.

Morton had finished his texting and he rose to his feet.

"It would seem, Your Honour, that this is a statement of conjecture rather than a question," said the defence counsel.

30

"Miss Buckingham?" queried Judge Clarke. He had that judicial knack of saying the same words on multiple occasions but each time they sounded and meant something entirely different.

Amanda turned back to the witness box. Smiling, she said, "You owe a lot to your two friends, don't you, Mr Toskas?"

"I have a great job, thanks to Ivan and Eddie," said Luca.

"Would I be right in thinking you'd do anything for them?" asked Amanda.

Archie was up like a rocket. "Your Honour!" he screeched.

Amanda said flatly, "No further questions" and sat down.

The defence counsel stared at Amanda. He shuffled his feet, pulled on the lapels of his gown and began his questioning.

"Mr Toskas, hello. I'm Mr Archie Morton and I want to ask you just one question."

Luca smiled as he hoped he'd soon to be out of the witness box.

"When you left Mr Derbyshire, Mr Delaney and Miss Tomkins to go further up the stairs, at the point when Mr Derbyshire told you to go back to the party, what was your impression about Miss Tomkins' attitude?"

"I do not understand the question," said Luca.

"Was it your impression that Miss Tomkins was going willingly with the two men?" rephrased the defence counsel.

"She was laughing and touching Ivan," he answered. "She was going up the stairs quite quickly; I know that because I was taking two steps at a time myself."

"No further questions," declared Archie as he sat down with a smugness that some barristers possess.

Amanda's re-examination was cursory. She knew that she had misjudged Luca and had, naively, not seen Archie's single question coming until it was too late.

Judge Clarke decided on an early finish. The jury were delighted until he kept everyone another ten minutes to explain that the members of the jury must not talk to anyone about the case or undertake any research in relation to the facts or the law.

As Amanda watched the two defendants depart, she was repulsed by the thumbs up Eddie Delaney gave to Archie. She spoke to the CPS solicitor outside the courtroom and, after a few perfunctory comments, they agreed that it was early days. She left the building through a side exit and switched on her mobile phone.

There were three messages and several emails, but she knew the one she would open first. She read the words carefully:

'R has an infection. On antibiotics. Not good. Lump was benign. B.'

Tuesday was a damp, mild June day. It started badly for the prosecution team and never recovered. Edward Delaney entered the witness box and promised to tell the truth. He radiated self-confidence. He agreed with everything that Amanda asked him.

Yes, he had gone up to the boardroom to have sex with Sarah. None of them had taken drugs although all three had consumed rather a lot of alcohol: in his case, he estimated seven cans of lager.

He confirmed that he was in awe of Ivan and would do anything for him. He liked Luca, and he thought that Sarah was "sensational". He did not deny that he had made a rather crude suggestion involving the two males but said that Sarah had applauded his idea. Amanda glanced to her left; Sarah was shaking her head in silent outrage.

She had chosen to attend the trial, and, at the pre-trial conference with the CPS, she agreed that she would not opt for any of the evidential special measures that were afforded to victims of sexual assaults. Sarah had also waived her right to give evidence by video-link even though the CPS solicitor had delicately explained that she might find being questioned in the witness box incredibly harrowing. Ultimately the CPS made the ruling, but Sarah confirmed it was the right thing to do. It was a courageous decision.

Amanda continued with her questioning of Eddie.

"Mr Delaney, I regret that I need to raise an unpleasant matter with you."

Eddie Delaney remained impassive.

"Do you deny that, at the end of your assault on..."

"If I may, Your Honour," cried out Archie Morton, "counsel is prejudging the decision of the jury. Her statement is grossly misleading."

Judge Clarke was displeased. He decided to reassert his authority.

"Miss Buckingham! I will not allow you any further leeway in this case. You will not again, in my court, make such a distorted statement." He turned to the jury and ordered them to disregard the question.

Amanda was stung by the judicial rebuke.

"I apologise, Your Honour," she said, sensing that she might have lost the momentum that she was carefully trying to build.

"Mr Delaney," she continued. "Did you, towards the end of the events in question, touch Miss Tomkins' inner thighs?"

"No," Delaney replied.

"No, Mr Delaney?" exclaimed Amanda incredulously. "May I remind you that you are under oath and you are required to tell the truth."

"I did not force myself on Sarah. She was gagging for it and she encouraged me." He paused and added, "She was laughing. She loved it."

There was total silence in the courtroom. Sarah Tomkins collapsed in tears into her mothers' arms. The judge allowed a few moments to elapse before indicating to Amanda that she should continue.

"What happened next?"

"I was wondering whether we might do other things," responded the witness.

"Other things?" asked Amanda.

"Well, she was having fun."

Sarah Tomkins put her hands over her face and wept silently.

Judge Clarke was not an uncaring or insensitive man. Realising that the emotions inside his courtroom had ratcheted up, and the increased tension had engulfed everyone like a noxious gas, he called a halt to proceedings and ordered that everyone would take an early lunch. He then asked both barristers into his Chambers. This style of judicial conference used to be quite commonplace but, with the various changes to legal processes, they now occur less often. When they do take place, what is said is added to the Digital Audio Recording Transcription and Storage court recording system – DARTS. Judge Clarke was careful in what he said to both barristers but he made it abundantly clear that he was growing displeased with their conduct. Both Amanda and Archie left, chastened, like two naughty schoolchildren exiting the headmaster's office.

When the court resumed, Archie Morton revisited all the previous evidence and managed to convey to Amanda and, in her view, the jury as well, Eddie Delaney's disbelief that Sarah was suggesting she had not participated willingly. By the end of the day's proceedings, the body language of several of the jury appeared to suggest that they were satisfied that the accused might be innocent.

The records of the police examiner were admitted without objection from either barrister so the third witness to take the stand was Dr Rebecca Atkinson.

Amanda took a line of questioning that proved to be a little too casual. She established that Dr Atkinson had been on duty at the Accident and Emergency Department of Nailton Hospital on the Friday night when the Heaton party had taken place. Dr Atkinson confirmed that she had examined the patient identified as Sarah Tomkins and had inserted three stitches inside her perineum. She had prescribed a course of antibiotics and later discharged the patient as they were desperately short of beds.

When asked the direct and final question, Dr Atkinson said that, in her medical opinion, the injuries, which included redness on the inner thighs, were consistent with a physical sexual assault.

Amanda left the last phrase hanging in the air and

invited her professional adversary to cross-examine the witness.

Archie Morton rose to his feet slowly and with deliberate purpose.

"Dr Atkinson," he began. "How long was it between Sarah Tomkins arriving at the Accident and Emergency Department and your examination taking place?"

"I can't be certain," replied the doctor. "We were very busy that evening. There had been a fire in the town centre and we had some patients needing help with breathing difficulties due to smoke inhalation."

"Quite," observed the weasel-like barrister. "Thank you for your helpful answer, Dr Atkinson. We accept the pressures you must face in your work. I will repeat my question. How long was it between Sarah Tomkins…?"

"I understand the question," snapped the doctor. "I think from memory it was about three hours which is within the government's target timings."

"Three hours," repeated the defence counsel. "Can we therefore conclude that the injuries sustained by Sarah Tomkins were not considered to be an emergency?"

"No," responded the doctor. "I work in the Emergency Department."

"You work, Dr Atkinson, in the Accident and Emergency Department. I put it to you that the injuries sustained by Sarah Tomkins were not an emergency. They were an accident, which you correctly and efficiently treated."

"She needed stitches," said the doctor. "She had been assaulted."

"We'll come on to that," said Archie. "If you had

not seen Sarah Tomkins for four hours, what would have been the medical consequences?"

"She needed stitches," replied Rebecca. "She had been assaulted."

"Dr Atkinson, it is not for you to say she had been assaulted." Archie paused to allow the jury to consider his words. "Shall we agree," he continued "that your patient was not an emergency? She needed hospital treatment which was non-urgent?"

"You're putting words in my mouth," replied Dr Atkinson.

Amanda was now realising that she had erred badly in not taking the doctor's evidence more seriously and that there should have been a lot more direct questioning as to the nature and extent of Sarah's injuries. On several occasions she went to challenge Archie Morton's questions but decided to wait.

"You have said that you inserted three stitches, Dr Atkinson. Where was that?"

"The perineum, at the entry of the vagina."

"How long is the vagina?" asked Archie Morton.

"It varies but shall we say about four inches in this patient's case."

"And where, Dr Atkinson, were the stitches inserted. How deep in did you have to go?" asked Archie.

"I inserted the injuries at the opening," replied the doctor.

"The opening," mused the defence counsel. "And why did you insert three stitches?"

"Your Honour," pleaded Amanda "There is simply no purpose in this line of questioning. We have accepted that Sarah Tomkins required three stitches."

"I'll permit the question," said Judge Clarke.

"Thank you, Your Honour." Archie Morton took a pace back and stared at the witness.

"Could Sarah Tomkins have managed with two stitches?" he asked.

"In my medical opinion..."

"Did the injury need stitches at all?" he said. "Was there internal bleeding?"

"There was no bleeding. There was a tear which, in my medical opinion, required stitches."

"Would you have endangered the patient if you had inserted two stitches?" asked Archie.

"In my medical opinion..."

"Thank you, Doctor Atkinson. How often do you come across this type of injury?"

"More often than you might imagine," said Dr Atkinson.

"Are you able to explain to the court the usual cause?" asked Archie.

"Oh. That's easy. The vagina is quite delicate and nearly always it's the result of physical intercourse taking place. It looks worse..."

The defence counsel was quite happy for the doctor to continue talking.

"...because injuries in what is a very sensitive area can bleed a lot during and after sex, due to the heart working harder."

"The result of sexual intercourse, Dr Atkinson. Between a man and a woman."

"Well, there are a number of variations but yes, heterosexual sex."

"Dr Atkinson. You have referred to Sarah Tomkins being assaulted. You witnessed the alleged assault, did you?"

"Of course not. The paramedics told us. It was written on her triage notes. It's also what the patient had told them."

"The injury you treated. Can you say with any certainty how it was caused?"

"It was consistent with a physical assault."

"Or was it consistent with normal consensual sexual intercourse?" asked Archie.

"Well, I suppose it could have been."

"Can you say, Dr Atkinson, with any degree of certainty, that, in your opinion, there was clear evidence that your patient had been physically assaulted?"

The witness hesitated.

Archie Morton stood, his eyes fixed on the witness stand and counted to ten in his head.

"Dr Atkinson," he continued. "Did your patient, Sarah Tomkins, tell you that she had been assaulted?"

"She didn't say very much at all and I had a heavy workload."

"I want to repeat your words, Dr Atkinson," said Archie. "'She didn't say very much'." Does that tell you anything?"

"Women who have been sexually assaulted usually react in one of two ways," replied the doctor. "Some, quite evidently, are distressed and traumatised. Others say absolutely nothing."

"And what does the reaction tell you?" asked Archie.

"Usually I'm afraid that I'm too busy tending to the medical needs of my patients to get too involved in their mental state." She paused. "If I feel a patient needs psychiatric support I will call in a colleague."

"Thank you, Dr Atkinson," smiled Archie. "What you are telling the ladies and gentlemen of the jury is that you were otherwise engaged with your medical duties and, in truth, you had little idea about Sarah Tomkins' emotional state."

"I wouldn't put it like that," replied the doctor.

"I want to ask you about the alleged damaged skin on her inner thighs," continued Archie. "What treatment did you administer? How many marks were there?" he asked.

"The skin was inflamed and red," said the doctor.

"And how many marks were there?"

"There were several impressions on the skin. They did not need treating although I did rub some cream into her body to help the healing."

Archie continued his questioning.

"Dr Atkinson. I only have two more questions for you. The redness, as you call it, on Sarah Tomkins's thighs. If that had been her only injury, how would you have treated it?"

"I have no way of knowing that," replied the witness. "She would never have reached me. A nurse would have seen her."

"Thank you," said Archie. "My final question. Can you please describe the condition of Sarah Tomkins when you first examined her?"

"She was lying on the bed. She was half asleep."

"When you talked to her, was she rational?"

"She asked if she could still have children."

"What was your answer, Dr Atkinson?"

"I was able to tell her that, as far as I could be certain, she was physically fine but she should see her own doctor if she wanted further reassurance."

"And you judged that physically, and emotionally,

she was ready to be discharged after you had treated her?"

"Yes. We needed the bed."

"No further questions, Your Honour," said Archie Morton.

Amanda knew that it was too late to undo the damage inflicted by Archie Morton's incisive cross examination. She was personally affronted, but professional impressed, by Archie's skilful approach.

She watched again as Eddie Delaney put up his thumb towards Archie and the visitor's gallery. She vaguely heard Judge Clarke closing the day's proceedings and again advising the jury that they were not to talk to any third party about the case.

Amanda put her papers in her case and sat down to think. She had the option of re-examining Dr Atkinson in the morning but she could see no advantage in doing this: there was little she could do now Archie had won the day. As she left the building she turned on her mobile phone. There were seven messages and three missed calls. Not one of them was from Ben.

The law student's tally chart, with marks out of ten, from the back of the public gallery, now read: *Not Guilty 6. Guilty 3.* He needed to work on his mathematics.

Amanda left the court building in need of carbs. Arriving back at her flat via the local pizza takeaway, her mobile phone vibrated.

'So sorry. R is struggling. We're fighting for him. B.'

Amanda went into her bedroom, stripped off her clothes and put on her cheongsam. She returned to the kitchen and ate a thin and crispy Hawaiian pizza with extra pineapple as if she had not eaten for days. She managed all but a few crusts and one solitary slice which she threw into the bin. She collected a bottle of chilled mineral water from the fridge, and walked to the sofa, where she had discarded her case notes minutes earlier.

Later she went to bed before midnight but didn't fall sleep until after two in the morning. She then had a dream. She was back in Kowloon with Fat Freddie or, rather, Fat Son Sue. He was telling her to work harder.

She made her first misjudgement on Wednesday morning by texting Trevor Hamper-Houghton to confirm their Saturday trip to Brussels. His curt reply of "Agreed" left her feeling a little emotionally empty.

Ivan Derbyshire proved to be a more challenging witness. He had clearly decided to say as little as possible and his repetition of "Yes" and "No" unsettled Amanda. He even prevaricated when giving the details of the deal he had secured for Heaton Van Sales and the commissions he had paid out of his bonus. In answer to the question "So you gave £200 to Sarah Tomkins?" he replied "Yes". When asked why he had done so, he said, "I wanted to".

Amanda took him through the events of the Friday evening: the party, the atmosphere, Sarah's disclosure that she suggested a more private party, the climb up the stairs, Eddie's role, his physicality, his shock at Sarah's injuries about which he had known nothing, and his concern for her well-being.

Amanda played her trump card.

"Mr Derbyshire. You have a partner and you live together."

"Yes."

"You have a son?"

"Yes. Billy."

"I understand that your partner is pregnant."

"Yes."

"How many weeks?"

"Twenty something, I think."

"Was it difficult for you to explain to your partner that you had been unfaithful?"

Archie Morton went to object and then sat down again.

"No," said Derbyshire.

"No!" repeated Amanda. "What is her name?"

"Debbie."

"Debbie," said Amanda. "What does Debbie think about what's happened? How does she feel about you standing here before this court?"

Archie Morton again went to protest at the question but sat down.

"Nothing," said Ivan.

"Nothing," said Amanda.

Ivan remained quiet.

"You are asking the jury to believe that your pregnant partner was relaxed about you having sex with a work colleague."

"She told me to."

"I beg your pardon, Mr. Derbyshire. Are you saying that Debbie encouraged you to have sex with another woman?"

"Yes," he said. "With Sarah."

Amanda turned to Judge Clarke.

"Your Honour, this witness simply cannot be trusted with this evidence."

"Continue with your questions, please, Miss

Buckingham," was the terse reply.

"Let me understand this exactly," said Amanda. "You are telling this court that your pregnant partner encouraged you to have sex with Sarah Tomkins?"

"Yes."

"Why?" asked Amanda.

"Debs is struggling. She's got high blood pressure. She understands that I need regular sex. She can't do it. She told me to shag Sarah. She worked at Heaton and said all the girls thought that Sarah was gagging for it."

The law student marked down another point for Not Guilty and then closed his note book.

Amanda lay on her sofa in complete silence. There was no music, no background sound and no cat. She went over and over the evidence she had heard during the last three days. There was no doubt in her mind that Ivan and Eddie had assaulted Sarah Tomkins. Sarah's behaviour had muddied the waters by dancing with Ivan and wanting to have sex with Ivan. However, Sarah had never expected Eddie to become involved and immediately she made it clear that she was not consenting, the two salesmen had broken the law.

Sarah had been determined so far, but tomorrow she would give her testimony, and Archie would tear her to pieces.

Amanda was worried. She had never lost a case before but she felt that might change tomorrow. She tried to sleep, she wanted it, she needed it but, as she drifted in and out of consciousness, she went back to her disagreement with the officer from the CPS.

"The   decision   to   prosecute   is   quite straightforward, Miss Buckingham," she had said. "It's a clear case of assault and rape. The girl said "No". There was no consent. There were her injuries. There was the damage to her body. She collapsed down the stairs and was lucky that the man caught her. All you have to do is persuade the jury that Sarah is telling the truth, not the defendants."

Amanda tossed and turned from side to side. She put her arm out to rub Rumpole's head but he was fighting for his life in the animal hospital.

In the early hours, Amanda woke from a fitful sleep and went over to the window. She looked at the lights of the twenty-four hour city beneath her. She turned back to the divan and sat down with a glass of water in her hand.

Her memory went back to her abortion. The five-star treatment at the private hospital and Eileen's love and care, which partly mitigated the pain and humiliation. She relived the event. Even Fat Freddie's judo training had not prepared her for a man of fifteen stones grabbing her from behind. He had seemed so caring and friendly. She accepted that they were moving towards the start of a relationship and she had arranged a doctor's appointment to ask for a prescription for birth control pills.

It was a sunny day and she drank too much wine. When his hand strayed too far up her thigh she told him to stop and he complied. She relaxed and a few moments later stood up and removed her skirt and blouse to reveal her bikini. That was naively provocative. Five minutes later he came on her from behind. She collapsed under the pressure of his weight and was unable to stop him penetrating her.

As they stood up and faced each other she suddenly executed a perfect *harai goshi*. The sweeping hip throw resulted in her assailant landing on his back with Amanda holding his arm which she was twisting against the joint.

"I am two inches away from breaking your shoulder," she said, before she released him and fled the scene.

What she did not do was to see the doctor and obtain a morning-after pill. It never occurred to her that she might be pregnant. She fought the increase in her weight until she started being sick in the mornings. Eileen knew immediately and booked an appointment for her to see a doctor at her own private clinic. Her uncle was not involved. She looked after her niece and rarely left her side. Her recovery from the termination was medically satisfactory and complete. Her aunt never once preached to her. She just hugged her.

The day before she was discharged from the hospital, she received a visitor. Anthony Buckingham, as always, looked immaculate. They discussed Tony Blair and the Conservative Party's inability to dislodge him. He moaned that his wife did not understand him and then winked at his niece.

He stood up to leave. As he reached the door he turned back.

"The chairman of a company," he began, "where I was marketing manager once saved my skin. I had dropped a huge clanger and he covered up for me. As I left his office after the biggest reprimand I had ever faced, he said to me, "Buckingham. Your gross incompetence is history. You judged the supplier on face value. You did not think things through. You did not check the facts. You can now only make one more error. If you fail to learn from your mistake you'll leave us." He paused before choosing his words, "I did learn and I prospered," he added.

As she stared at the closing door, Amanda made a vow to herself. She would learn from her mistakes. It was a lesson she was never to forget.

After she returned to her bed, she continued to slumber into the early hours. She inevitably thought further about Sarah Tomkins. She went over and over the events of the Heaton party. She wanted to be sure that she was not judging things on face value. At five-fifteen in the morning she received a text message and immediately pictured Rumpole alone in the animal hospital. She got out of bed and went into the lounge. She then read the brief request:

'Is it too early to chat? THH.'

She pressed his number and immediately heard his voice.

"Just wondered how your case was going?" he asked.

Amanda lay back on her bed and tried to avoid an adverse reaction from her friend because she was trying to look forward to their planned Saturday trip into Europe. It was not too long before Trevor was testing her. He explained that he had been in Chambers the previous afternoon (and he did not fail to mention that he had won a case against the Inland Revenue for one of their clients who had become involved in a dubious film financing scheme) and picked up comments that she was not handling the sexual assault too well. He then added to Amanda's angst by suggesting he might be able to advise her on her courtroom strategy.

Amanda proceeded to go through the key points of the case with him and was reassured that he did not interrupt or make any comment apart from the occasional "oh boy". When she had completed her summation, she admitted that she was nervous about putting Sarah Tomkins in the witness box.

"That's your big chance. Tell me about the jury," said Trevor.

Amanda went through the make-up: the six men and the six women.

"Pity," he concluded. "You need at least eight or nine women," he said.

"I know," admitted Amanda.

"Well, good luck. What approach will you be taking later?" he asked.

"I will try to show that she is a lovely woman who was assaulted. I shall focus on her evidence that she said "No"."

He interrupted her.

"Hang on, I want to top up my coffee."

Amanda used the interval to decide if their call was positive.

"Right. Back on duty," she heard him say. "Did you know that they call you 'AB' in the office? I'm going to call you 'AB'," he said. "Not very original I grant you, but it suits."

Did she just feel her heart race? For THH it was a rare moment of flirtatious banter.

"Well, BB," she said, "how would you handle Sarah?"

"BB?" he asked.

"Brilliant Barrister," she laughed.

"AB meets BB. Read all about it," he chuckled.

Amanda was enjoying their exchange. She really did wonder if THH might develop into something more real. Their similar legal backgrounds were a good start. She just wished he'd ask her more questions about herself.

"I would keep it short," he said. "You want the jury to be left with just one memory: she said "No"."

"And what about what Edward Delaney did to her?"

"I leave justice to the kingdom of heaven," said Trevor. "Good luck and let me know," and with that he terminated the call.

She went into the shower and turned the water to its hottest level. He was right. She realised that she was siding with Sarah and ignoring the facts. She knew that she only had one real opportunity to influence the jury. Sarah had said "No" and that is rape.

She dried herself and put on a tracksuit. She cycled on her machine for twenty minutes and felt awful. Her breakfast consisted of half a cup of filter coffee. Thursday was starting badly.

She re-read the message on her mobile phone:

'R very poorly. Trying different treatment. We're fighting for him. B.'

As she reached the court she ran into Judge Clarke. He nodded and hurried on into his Chambers.

Later that morning, Sarah Tomkins strode confidently to the witness box, Amanda silently applauded her. She was wearing a demure grey suit, no make-up, a hair band and low heels.

At first, Amanda concentrated on her early career at Heaton Van Sales and her success in becoming head receptionist. When Sarah let slip that, last year, the company had allowed her time off to nurse her dying grandmother, Amanda was in like an Exocet missile. By the time she was finished, she had portrayed Sarah as a humane, selfless and caring person.

They covered the events of the Friday party, her willingness to have sex with Ivan and her initial enthusiasm as they climbed the stairs to the boardroom.

Amanda was heading for the key moment if she was to convince the jury of the defendants' guilt. She enabled Sarah to exhibit her utter horror when she realised that she was expected to have sex with a second man, her punitive treatment on the boardroom table and her repugnancy at the physical pain inflicted by Eddie.

"Miss Tomkins," said Amanda as she faced the jury. "Did you, or did you not, agree to have sex with Edward Delaney?"

"No, I did not," replied Sarah in a clear and confident voice.

"Did you use that word, 'No'? Is that what you said?"

"That is what I said both to Ivan and to Eddie. I said "No" and I meant no."

"No further questions," said Amanda, as she returned to her seat. She studied the faces of the jury members. She was convinced that she had sowed the seeds of doubt in several of their minds.

Whereupon Archie Morton rose to his feet with the deliberation of a man convinced of his own importance and he proceeded to attack the creditability of Sarah Tomkins.

"Your Honour, members of the jury, I must start my cross examination of this witness with an apology. My job is to defend my clients to the best of my humble abilities and is to prevent a possible miscarriage of justice. My two clients, Ivan Derbyshire and Edward Delaney, are two hard-working and successful businessmen who were seduced by a colleague at an office party. We, here today, are all worldly-wise and this type of liaison occurs up and down this great country of ours. So, all that is needed, members of the jury, is to deal with just one matter."

Amanda's instinct was telling her that the mother of all bombs was about to be detonated in the courtroom.

"Miss Tomkins," he exploded, "I wish I did not have to ask you this question." He paused with superb timing. "Do you regularly have sex with married men, or men who have longer-term partners?"

Sarah tried desperately to retain her dignity.

"I consider that an unfair question," she replied.

"Miss Tomkins," continued Archie Morton. "Do you have sex with men who effectively are cheating on another person?"

Amanda was on her feet but Judge Clarke took no notice and so she sat down.

"Eddie forced himself on me," she pleaded.

"Miss Tomkins, how many times have you had sex with a married or committed man?"

"Amanda was up on her feet. "Your Honour, this has nothing to do with this…" Her words were lost as Judge Clarke intervened

"The witness will please answer the question.

Continue with your questions, Mr Morton."

"I'm obliged, Your Honour," he said. "Miss Tomkins. Let's take this step by step." He smiled at the witness. "Can we assume that you usually know the marital status of the men with whom you have sex?"

"Yes," said Sarah in a hushed voice. "One or two pull the wool, but you usually know."

"And do you perform vigorous sexual acts in your relationships with the men with whom you choose to have a relationship?"

"Some men make demands, yes," said Sarah.

"And can we assume that you perform these acts willingly?"

"It is part of love-making," she said, as Amanda wanted the floor to open up and swallow her whole.

"Do men ever force themselves on you?" asked the defence counsel.

Amanda rose and held out her hands in exasperation.

Judge Clarke took off his glasses.

"Mr Morton. I must admit I am wondering if you are beginning to push my patience and that of this court."

"Thank you, Your Honour," he said as he nodded. He then paused with magnificent effect. "If Your Honour will allow me to reach my crucial question?"

"As quickly as you can, please Mr Morton," replied the judge.

"I am most grateful, Your Honour."

"Miss Tomkins," he barked. "How many times have you had sex with a married man?"

"I honestly don't know," she said. Amanda looked at her feet.

"You don't know," repeated Archie Morton. "Let me try to help you, Miss Tomkins. "Shall we agree more than ten times?"

"I can't remember. Possibly."

"Twenty times," said Archie.

"You are trying to show me in a way that is not me," said Sarah.

"I am trying to show you as a woman who enjoys casual sex," said Archie.

"No," shouted Sarah. "Never. The partners I chose are all..."

"Are all what?" asked the defence counsel.

Amanda remained seated.

"Eddie raped me," said Sarah.

"No, Miss Tomkins. That is not true. You consented to the events that took place by admitting you wanted sex, by rushing up the stairs, by leading the way with two men into the boardroom, by having intercourse with Ivan while Eddie watched, and then having sex with Eddie." He paused and turned to the jury. "That is what happened, isn't it, Miss Tomkins?" He didn't wait for an answer.

"Just one more question, Miss Tomkins. And this puzzles me. You have told this court that you willingly went up to the boardroom to have sex with Ivan Derbyshire. As you reached the room you realised that Edward Delaney was to be involved." He paused. "Why, Miss Tomkins, why did you not simply walk away and none of the subsequent events would have taken place?"

Amanda knew the answer to the question. Sarah was aroused and wanted sex with Ivan. "Say nothing," Amanda thought to herself.

"I wish I had," shouted Sarah.

"Had what, Miss Tomkins?" asked Archie.

""Walked away", as you put it," she said.

"So, the members of the jury can base their decision on your evidence that you were in that boardroom willingly?"

"I said "No"!" shouted Sarah, defiantly.

Amanda decided to leave it at this point. She felt there would be no purpose served by re-examining the witness. She wanted the last thing ringing in the jurors' ears to be the word 'no'.

Not Guilty 8. Guilty 2. The law student considered not bothering to waste the bus fare again tomorrow as this case was all but over.

She returned to her flat alone and lonely. There were no messages from Ben and Trevor had not phoned her. The night hours seemed endless as she sat in court imagining the summary that Judge Clarke would deliver later the next morning. The two rapists would walk away laughing with their families and friends and go to the pub to celebrate their acquittal. Sarah would sneak away to a humiliating return to the reception desk at Heaton Van Sales, her reputation in tatters.

Her eyes were closing and she was drifting. She simply had no further stamina left to review the four days of evidence. She found herself dreaming about being in the Sung Wong Toi Park in Kowloon and there was Fat Freddie – both of them. They were each holding her hand. They sat down and Freddie Wing Wey turned to her and smiled.

"Ben niao xian fei zao ru lin," he said.

A clumsy bird that flies first will get to the forest earlier.

She woke up and was immediately alert.

"What, Fat Freddie. What is it? What am I missing?" she cried out.

She ran her hand through her hair and then she remembered something. She leaped out of bed, catching her foot in the duvet. She hit the floor with a shudder. It only momentarily impeded her progress. She dashed to her desk where she opened her papers and searched for Monday's notes. She then re-read several police files. She was becoming animated as she sensed a lead. She turned over each page, skim-reading the contents, and then she went back to one particular section. She found the passage she was looking for and then she located the later testimony. She checked and re-checked. She went on to where Sarah had fallen. It was all there and she had failed to realise its significance.

She rushed to the bathroom and threw cold water over her face.

"It's the hair. It's the colour of her bloody hair," she shouted out.

As his driver weaved his way through the Friday morning commuter traffic, Judge Maynard Clarke relaxed back into the cushioned rear seat of his judicial car and reflected on the readings which his monitor had recorded earlier in the morning. "147/85," he pondered. During a recent annual medical examination, his doctor had noted raised blood pressure. Before starting prescriptive treatment, he suggested that his patient, in order to eliminate 'white coat syndrome' (the stress of the doctor's surgery resulting in misleading results), buy a home monitor and record his BP each morning and again at the end of the day (but before the evening consumption of malt whisky).

His Honour knew that the systolic value (the reading showing the pressure as the blood leaves the heart through the arteries) was too high. He was pleased that the diastolic figure at '85', showing the pressure as the blood returns to the heart through the veins, was at a healthier level.

An hour later, in his room at the Nailton Crown Court, as he stared at Amanda Buckingham, had his blood pressure been taken, both readings would almost certainly have been considerably raised.

Archie Morton was frustrated and concerned. He had been caught completely off guard with the CPS's application to recall an earlier witness. Archie had tried to say 'no' but he had no idea what he was saying 'no' to or why he wanted to say 'no'. After a lot of multi-syllable verbosity his main reason for objecting was because the CPS had asked.

"I grant the application Miss Buckingham," declared Judge Clarke, "but be under no misapprehension: I can give you no latitude with your questions."

The CPS and Amanda had achieved the requisite permission from Judge Clarke but it took several hours for the court officials and the police to locate the individual and bring him back to court.

At 11.59 on Friday morning of the trial of Ivan Derbyshire and Edward Delaney, the man stared out of the witness box looking bewildered and anxious. He confirmed his name and that he understood he was still under oath. He watched as Amanda Buckingham approached him.

"Mr Toskas," she said.

Despite all the events of the last five days, Judge

Clarke secretly admired the prosecuting counsel. In his assessment, she had that special quality that marked her down as a barrister with a future.

"Mr Toskas," she repeated. "I want to revisit some of the evidence you gave to this court last Monday."

"I told the truth," he spluttered.

"Mr Toskas," she continued. "During the events of the Friday night party at Heaton Van Sales you told this court that you followed Ivan Derbyshire, Edward Delaney and Sarah Tomkins out of the staff canteen and up the stairs."

"I told the truth. Ivan told me to piss off and so I went back to the party."

"Yes. I am satisfied that you have correctly confirmed what you said."

"Your Honour," interrupted Archie Morton. "Where is this meaningless line of questions taking us?" he said.

"Sit down, Mr Morton," ruled the judge "Miss Buckingham. Please speed up your questioning."

"Thank you, Your Honour," said Amanda.

She looked down at her notes.

"Mr Toskas," she continued. "Did you tell this court that you returned to a particular girl."

Luca Toskas put his hands to his face.

"Yes," he said.

"What is her name?"

"Chaudra," he replied.

"And what colour hair does she have?" asked Amanda.

"Your Honour," angered Archie Morton, "this is a farce. We'll be told the name of her hairdresser if prosecuting counsel continues this approach."

"Miss Buckingham, I really can't permit your line

of questioning much longer."

"Thank you, Your Honour," said Amanda.

She turned and faced the witness box.

"Mr Toskas. You have said that you returned to the party to be with a special girl. Yes or no?"

"Yes, Chaudra. She's dark-haired," he answered. "She is beautiful."

"Can I confirm that, please Mr Toskas? Chaudra is dark-haired. A brunette."

"Yes," said the witness.

"Yes," repeated the prosecution counsel. "That is what you said to the police officer who interviewed you on the evening of the party. He specifically recorded her name and that she was dark-skinned and a brunette." Amanda paused.

"So why did you tell this court that she was blonde?"

Luca reddened in his face. He looked down and started to fidget.

"I don't remember," he spluttered. "Chaudra is dark. She is what I told you. I can't have said that."

"Shall I have the recording of your evidence given last Monday played back to the members of the jury?" asked Amanda.

"P-perhaps I said she was blonde," muttered an increasingly desperate Luca.

But the wheels were coming off. He tried to argue that he could not tell the difference between the two colours, that Chaudra often changed the colour of her hair and that he had been confused.

Finally, Amanda pounced.

"Mr Toskas. I put it to you that, in fact, you did not go down the stairs, but you waited and, after a few moments in time, you went up the stairs?"

Tears filled his eyes.

"Please. I'm so sorry. I'm going to church every day to ask for forgiveness. I am so sorry".

"Why are you so sorry?" asked Amanda. "Why, Mr Toskas?" she repeated.

He looked across the court room towards the two defendants.

"I can't tell you. Eddie will beat me up," he said.

She now took the terrified witness, step by step, thought the events of the Friday evening. He had waited for several minutes before following the three participants up the stairs. He said that he wanted to know what happened. When he reached the third floor the door was closed but the window blind had not been fully lowered. He had watched the events with a clear view. He said he could see and hear everything.

When Eddie had left the room, he had hidden along the corridor and then, moments later, watched Ivan leave. He looked into the room and saw that Sarah was sitting in a chair. He went down the stairs and then heard her open the door. As he turned around and looked up the stairs he found her collapsing into his arms. He said that there was blood on her hand.

"Mr Toskas," said Amanda. "I want you please to think carefully about my next question. When Sarah was struggling on the table, and being held down, did you hear her say anything?"

"She was fighting to get free. Ivan was holding her down."

"Did she say anything?" asked Amanda.

"She shouted out "No!"," said the witness.

"Are you sure? Could she have said 'oh'?" asked

Amanda.

"No. She said "No" and then Eddie hit her. He and Ivan were like animals. She was in terrible trouble."

Eddie leaped up and threw himself at the protection screen that guarded the defendants from the open courtroom.

"Luca. You're a fucking dead man walking," he bellowed. Amanda stood in horror as the real Edward Delaney presented himself to the world. He looked deranged. His eyes bulged; the veins in his neck looked like they were trying to force their way out of his skin. Several of the jury recoiled.

Eddie thumped the screen and spittle dripped down like rain on a windscreen.

Eventually he was restrained by the court officials. When sense returned he slumped down into seat with the heaviness of a man who knows he's in serious trouble.

After that, events moved quickly. The defendants changed their plea and admitted to the offences with which they were charged in order to try and mitigate their custodial sentences.

Their families and friends emptied from the visitor's gallery and never returned.

The law student sat, open mouthed, his eyes flitting back and forth in disbelief at what he had just witnessed. He never updated his tally score. He was glad he had made a late decision to return to the courtroom.

Judge Clarke thanked and dismissed the jury, remanded the prisoners in custody and deferred sentencing until two weeks' time. He warned Ivan

Derbyshire and Edward Delaney that they faced custodial sentences.

As the court rose, Amanda caught the eye of the Judge. There was hardly a flicker of recognition but there was, perhaps, an imperceptible nod of his head. Archie Morton refused to acknowledge his peer and stormed out of the building.

Amanda later spoke to her Chambers. She was told that there was a bundle of papers being couriered to her home detailing a case of death by dangerous driving starting at the magistrate's court on Monday morning. To her relief she was defending the motorist. As she headed for her car she checked again and felt disappointed that there was no message about her cat.

There was, however, a text from Sarah Tomkins asking if they could meet. Reluctantly, Amanda decided to agree. She felt that the receptionist had been through so much over the last few weeks. It was an ill-advised move but she said she would see her in the park later in the afternoon. She knew that the fresh air would do her good in the light of another text message she had received:

'Well done AB. Sorry, but u're not my type. Let's move on. THH.'

She spoke just one word: "Diu."

As they later came together in the open spaces Amanda felt a sense of admiration for her.

"Thank you for agreeing to meet with me," said Sarah. "I'm a bit tearful but at least it's all over."

"Briefly, Sarah," said Amanda "and then you must never contact me again."

They walked together along a tree-lined path. They

watched as two dogs chased each other.

"Did you hear that Debbie Derbyshire lost her baby last night?" she asked.

Amanda said nothing. She allowed a period of silence to continue.

"You know I can't find the words," said Sarah.

"I did my job," said Amanda.

"I wanted to tell you my news," said Sarah. She ignored the silence. "I'm going to train as a social worker. When I nursed my Gran last year I found something I wanted to do. I'm going to study to be a manager of a care home."

"Sounds good," said Amanda. "The cut in pay will hurt."

"I have all the money I need, I'm to receive a decent pay-off,'" said Sarah. "Mr Heaton, the chairman, phoned me from his holiday home." He had listened carefully to the advice given to him by Yvette, the personnel director.

Amanda paused. She wanted to know something.

"Sarah, what will happen to Luca?" she asked.

"Unbelievable. The lads from the office collected him and took him back to the depot. He was kissed by all the girls." She paused. "A particular brunette took charge of him."

"Chaudra," said Amanda.

Sarah laughed.

"Justice has won the day. Isn't that right, Amanda?" Before the barrister could reply she went on, "Did you know that a clerk from accounts has gone to the police? She's claiming she was also raped by Ivan and Eddie."

Amanda winced. She took Sarah's left hand and squeezed it.

They shared a fond, almost sisterly, embrace and, as Sarah walked away, Amanda watched her go.

As she turned towards the Tube station her phone vibrated. She looked down at the message:

'He's better. He's has had small meal. One more night to be sure. Collect him tomorrow mid-morning. B.'

She stood still, beaming, and then skipped down the stairs into the underground station. As she neared her Clerkenwell flat there was a further text message from Ben.

Ivan Derbyshire and Edward Delaney were sentenced to five and seven years in prison. Eddie took to the brutal regime like a duck to water and began to make several questionable associates. Ivan became reclusive and needed medical help for depression. He was not helped by the disappearance of Debbie who, once she had been discharged from hospital following the loss of her baby, relocated to the Lake District with her son. She found work in a Windermere restaurant and, within a year, she had begun a new relationship and became pregnant. She never saw Ivan again.

During the investigation at Heaton Van Sales, the police uncovered a discrepancy in the sales invoice for the van transaction, which had triggered the party. It was later revealed that the money due to be paid was being collected by a Guernsey-based associated company and HMRC tax inspectors were undertaking a comprehensive audit and review. Not long after, the chairman was back in the country facing prosecution for VAT-related fraud. The business subsequently went into liquidation and was bought out by a competitor. The girls on reception all survived but, by now, Luca had left. He and Chaudra emigrated to

Italy to begin a new life together.

Sarah Tomkins decided to fly to Portugal for a week in the sun. She was soon talking to the man sitting in the window seat and they arrived at Faro in a decidedly relaxed manner. He was into property sales and Sarah accepted his invitation for her to visit him at his villa. After a repeat trip several weeks later, this became a more permanent arrangement. She remained in close contact with her mother and tried to persuade her to join her and her new partner in the Iberian sunshine.

Archie Morton reacted petulantly to the loss of the case but quickly recovered and was soon back in court. Judge Maynard Clarke overcame his blood pressure problems by adopting a vegetarian diet and losing two stone in weight.

Early on the Saturday morning following the end of the trial, Zach put Amanda through her paces in the boxing ring and insisted she swam forty lengths of the pool. She feasted on bowls of fresh fruit and figs. She returned home and decided to wear her hair loose, a white shirt and jeans.

She arrived at the vets late in the morning. Ben brought Rumpole out to her in his cage. He immediately tried to lick her fingers which she had pushed through the wire cover.

She turned to the vet.

"I received your text message," she said.

Ben looked at her.

"You've a spare ticket for the theatre, tonight," she laughed.

Ben said nothing.

"I think I can consent to that," she smiled.

As she put her cat in the back of her car, she realised that she had no idea what they were going to see.

THE END

NOTE: THE STORY OF 'THE ACCUSED'

This 1988 American drama was one of the first Hollywood films to include a rape incident of unimaginable graphic realism.

The storyline for *The Accused* was loosely based on the 1983 gang rape of Cheryl Araujo in New Bedford, Massachusetts and the resulting trial. This film is set in Washington State but was filmed in Vancouver, Canada.

Sarah Tobias (played by Jodie Foster) is gang raped in a bar.

Assistant District Attorney Kathryn Murphy (played by Kelly McGillis), agrees a plea bargain with the legal representatives of the three men accused. They plead guilty to a charge of 'reckless endangerment' which carries a lesser prison sentence and the chance of parole. Sarah is incensed, not least because she was denied the opportunity to testify in court.

Kathryn opts to prosecute three witnesses identified by a friend of Sarah. They are charged with criminal solicitation. The evidence in court is partly overlaid with a visual reproduction of the whole of the rape scene. Another bystander gives evidence and the three men are convicted. One consequence is that the perpetrators, now in prison, will serve longer sentences and not be eligible for parole.

The final scene is a display, by Sarah and Kathryn, of mutual respect as they go their separate ways.

+

The French-born director, Jonathan Kaplan, was a

protégé of Martin Scorsese and made *Truck Tuner* in 1974. He continued actively although it was his 1988 film 'The Accused' that was one of his most critically acclaimed works. He now concentrates mostly on TV films.

Kelly McGillis's distinguished career includes *Witness* (1985) with Harrison Ford and *Top Gun* (1986) with Tom Cruise. In 1982, she and her live-in girlfriend were assaulted and raped by two men in her New York apartment. For this reason, she turned down the part of Sarah Tobias in *The Accused* but agreed to play the Assistant District Attorney, Kathryn Murphy. She lives in North Carolina and teaches acting.

Jodie Foster is considered to be one of the best actresses of her generation. Her breakthrough came with Martin Scorsese's *Taxi Driver*. She was not an immediate choice for the role of Sarah Tobias in *The Accused* but went on to win an Academy Award. She then played Clarice Starling in *The Silence of the Lambs*. She now concentrates on film directing.

AMANDA BUCKINGHAM: AN EARLY HISTORY

Amanda was born on 3 June 1983 on Kowloon Island, Hong Kong. She was an only child and registered as being British. Her father, Arthur Grosvenor Marin Buckingham, was deputy head of the civil service in the Territory. He played a pivotal role in negotiating the handover from Britain to China.

These were turbulent times, with anti-British riots and bombings which were encouraged by the Chinese authorities. There was an influx of Vietnamese refugees of whom, by 1988, there were 50,000 on the island. There were continuing fears that the Chinese would abandon their commitment to their 'one country, two systems' pledge. The transfer of sovereignty eventually took place in 1997 when Amanda was fourteen years old.

Her early years were dominated by her father's descent into heavy drinking and libidinous behaviour. She was the product of a brief dalliance with a hotel receptionist, Julie Neo, a Hong Kong citizen. Her father died the day after the transfer of Hong Kong to China by the British government.

Amanda was educated at the Diocesan School for Girls in Hong Kong learning Cantonese and later French much to the annoyance of her father. After his death it was decided, in conjunction with the British authorities, that Amanda should move to London.

She arrived with a dual passport and a trust fund of several million pounds. Her uncle, and a firm of London solicitors, were the trustees. She knew that she would be eligible for half the money when she reached twenty-one years of age and the balance when she was thirty.

She took her time and spent the early days with her aunt, Eileen and her step-brother, Jonathan, who both amused and irritated her in equal measure. Her uncle was rarely at home.

Her academic record, including twelve GCSE's and four A-Levels including Law, resulted in her achieving entrance to Lady Margaret Hall, Oxford, including a year at Pantheon-Assas, in Paris. In 2005, she graduated with a First Class, Oxon in Law (Jurisprudence). She included European Constitutional Law in her areas of expertise.

After coming down from Oxford University Amanda sailed through the Bar Vocational Course. A pupillage was secured for her at Hartington Chambers, a leading London criminal law set, Amanda was called to the Bar in 2007.

THE NOVELLA NOSTALGIA SERIES

We first meet Amanda in the second novella forming a series of titles inspired by iconic cinema classics. In *Twelve Troubled Jurors* she is the defence barrister and is mentioned only twice as most of the action takes place in the jury room.

In novella seven, *The Courageous Witness*, Amanda is the central character as she reprises the role played by Kelly McGillis in the film 'The Accused'.

ABOUT THE AUTHOR

After spending over a decade as a lawyer Oliver runs
a dispute resolution consultancy that helps businesses
resolve their commercial disputes through dialogue
and negotiation. He is Chairman of Bedfordshire's
region of Wooden Spoon, a charity that helps socially,
mentally and physically disadvantaged children and he
is also a volunteer at a local homeless outreach
organisation. He lives in Bedford with his wife and
daughter.

Oliver published his first novella, *Gloriana*, which is inspired by the Tom Cruise film, *Valkyrie*, in September 2018. Using the background of 'Brexit', *Gloriana* is a thunderous political thriller with an unexpected twist in the tale and it has received critical acclaim with many four and five star reviews on Amazon.

The Courageous Witness is his second novella and launches the career of mesmeric barrister Amanda Buckingham.

In addition to all of this Oliver is also writing a novel!

Contact Oliver:

Instagram	@oliverrichbell
Facebook	oliverjamesrichbell
Twitter	@richbelloliver

17958389R00043

Printed in Great Britain
by Amazon